Written by Stephen Cosgrove
Illustrated by Charles Reasoner

HAPPINESS BOOKS, INC.
Baltimore, Maryland 21208
1984

THIRD PRINTING – JULY 1984

Copyright© 1983 by Price/Stern/Sloan Publishers, Inc.
Published by Price/Stern/Sloan Publishers, Inc.
410 North La Cienega Boulevard, Los Angeles, California 90048

ISBN: 0-8431-1206-9

Dedicated to my brother Michael G.,
who, over breakfast, showed me
where the Blamberries grow.

Stephen

As you lay on a hot summer's day
In a cool and shady place,
Don't look up into the skies;
Instead, look down
And squint your eyes.
Squint them both so very tight
That if you look
With all your might
You'll find the land of
Morethansmall.
And in this land are buggs,
that's all.

The streets of Buggville seemed to roar and growl with the almost animal-like sounds of all the vehicles of all the buggs of Buggville. Some of the buggs raced up and down the park in motorized two-wheeled buggcycles, while another delivered the groceries to the Buggon Inn in an old bugg-bed truck.

The engines of all the bugg vehicles didn't run on gasoline; rather, they were fueled by filling the tanks with common water from Old Skunk Swamp. When the tanks were filled to the brim, each bugg driver would drop one powerful berry from the Blamberry Bush into the tank. Blam! Just like that, the engine would fire up and they'd be off to the races again.

The powerful Blamberries only grew out in parched lands called the Desert of the Dunes. They were grown under the watchful eyes of the nomadic Dune Buggs, who had wandered the deserts since time began.

It was in the shade of the great Blamberry Bush that the Dune Buggs would pitch their multi-colored tents. They would nurture the berries, pick them, pack them and sell them to the buggs in Buggville.

Every Wednesday, at precisely two o'clock, the buggbed truck from Buggville would pull up to the shade of the Blamberry Bush and the driver would buy all the Blamberries the Dune Buggs had picked that week.

Most of the Dune Buggs loved their life in the desert. It was there that they could ride the hump-back beetles freely across the sand dunes and bask in the warmth of the sun. Sometimes, though, they would just sit in the shade of the Blamberry Bush, and watch the golden sands reflect the light like millions of tiny diamonds.

All would have been content except for one sneaky, foxy, money-grubbing Dune Bugg called Prince Imagreedy.

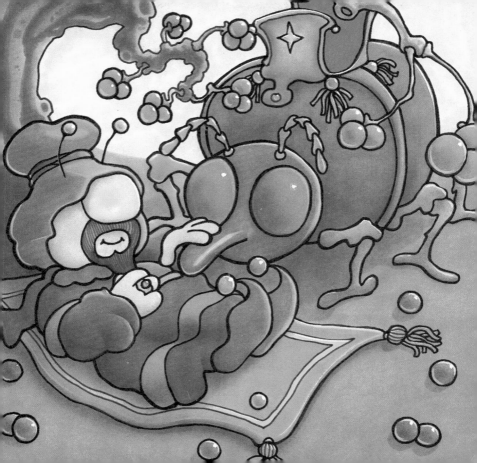

One day the prince decided that he had to have more money. When the truck arrived from Buggville to pick up the Blamberries, Prince Imagreedy said, "You must pay double what you normally pay for the Blamberries!"

The driver of the truck looked at him in total amazement, "You've got to be kidding! There's no way I'll pay double."

"All right," said the prince, with a sly smile. "Then you shall pay four times what you normally pay!"

The driver was furious but because there were no other Blamberries he finally paid the price and drove back to town.

Every Wednesday from then on when the truck would come out to pick up the Blamberries, Prince Imagreedy would raise the price just a little more. Week after week and month after month he did it, until finally one Wednesday the truck didn't come at all. All the Dune Buggs waited and waited but instead of the truck driving in from Buggville the driver rode up in a beetle-drawn cart.

The prince screamed that because he was so late the Blamberries would cost him ten times what he had paid last week. The driver just shook his head and said that they wouldn't need Blamberries anymore.

It seemed that the Blamberries had gotten so expensive that the buggs of Buggville couldn't afford to buy them. Without the Blamberries their cars wouldn't run and without their cars they didn't need the Blamberries. It was all very simple.

Prince Imagreedy didn't believe what he had heard. So he leaped on his hump-back beetle and raced to town. Sure enough, all of the cars and trucks were parked all over Buggville. The buggs were getting about town in wagons, carts and even by buggy.

As the prince stood there, trying to figure out what to do, up walked Mayor Buggwig. "Ahem, Prince Iamgreedy. We must have those Blamberries. For, as you see, we have no way to power the fire engine, the police car or our ambulance. But we have no more money left to pay you."

The prince looked about and then a sly smile whisked across his face. "If you can't afford to pay, maybe in exchange my fellow Dune Buggs and I can live for free at the Buggon Inn and you can owe us the rest."

The mayor thought for a moment as he looked at all the motorized vehicles parked in the street. "It's blackmail," he said reluctantly, "but we agree!"

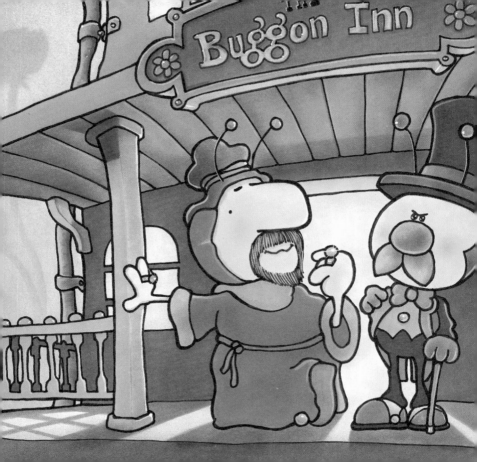

The very next day all of the Dune Buggs moved, bag and baggage, into the rooms at the Buggon Inn. Some of the other Buggs, like General Dewlittle, who lived there already, had to move out to make room for the Dune Buggs.

Day after day after day the Dune Buggs ran in, out and over the Buggon Inn as the townbuggs looked on in disbelief.

One day, as Mayor Buggwig was out walking, he looked up see Eevil Weevil drive by in his beat-up, junk jalopy. "Hold it!" the mayor shouted at the top of his lungs.

Eevil Weevil stepped quickly on the brakes and the jalopy clattered to a stop. "What do you want?" he grumbled as the mayor ran up.

"Where in the world," gasped the mayor, "did you find Blamberries for fuel?"

Eevil Weevil scratched his dusty head and said, "Oh, those. I don't use Blamberries. I just fill up my tank with water from Old Skunk Swamp." With that he clanked his car back into gear and roared out of Buggville in a cloud of black smoke.

The Mayor stood there in the dust for a moment or two before he realized what Eevil-Weevil had said. The Blamberries don't do anything. It was the water from Old Skunk Swamp!

The mayor was furious at the Prince's deception. He and the other buggs marched over to the Buggon Inn and threw them out, one and all. The Dune Buggs weren't sad about moving out. It was boring at the hotel and they happily went back to their beautiful golden desert.

The buggs of Buggville filled their vehicles to the brim with water from Old Skunk Swamp and with a roar and a pop and a puff, Buggville was motorized again.

If you try to sell some things
For more than they're worth to you
Remember the desert dune buggs
And say maybe Imagreedy too

What happened to Prince Imagreedy,
you ask. Well, I'll give you the real
scoop . . .

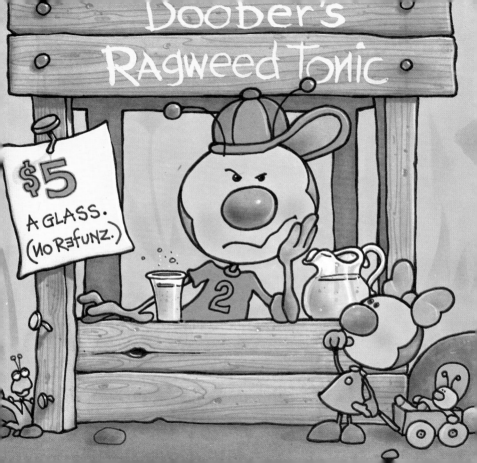

He spent the rest of his days eating sour Blamberry soup.